SCHEHERRYZADE
AND THE
ARABIAN NIGHTS

Story by Constance Allen
Text by Liza Alexander
Illustrations by Tom Brannon

A SESAME STREET/GOLDEN PRESS BOOK
Distributed by Western Publishing Company, Inc.
in conjunction with Children's Television Workshop

Once upon a time, in a land called Arabia, there lived a grouchy Queen. Even the laws she made were grouchy. In fact, one day she was feeling so grouchy that she banished bedtime stories throughout the land.

The grouchy new law made the townspeople very unhappy. How could their children be expected to go to bed without stories?

The brave Scheherryzade spoke up. He had a plan! He would try to persuade the Queen to take back her command.

That night Scheherryzade
visited the grouchy Queen. He
told her he knew a very exciting
story, and started to tell it.

But then he remembered that the Queen had forbidden stories. Too late! She was already interested.

The Queen ordered Scheherryzade to tell the tale.

Scheherryzade began to tell the story once more. It went like this:

Once upon a time, there lived a brave sailor named Sinbad who sailed the seven seas!

One day, Sinbad's ship ran aground on a giant
fish! The giant fish sneezed, and Sinbad was tossed
into the sea!

Scheherryzade stopped his story and yawned. He was too sleepy to go on. But the Queen had to know if Sinbad was okay! She made Scheherryzade promise to come back the next day and continue his story.

So the next day Scheherryzade continued to tell the tale. It went like this:

As Sinbad cried for help, a big wave came and swept the sailor far from his ship. The brave sailor floated around for some time. Then he spotted an island.

Soon after Sinbad waded ashore, he bumped into a large, round object. He wondered what it could be.

Suddenly, an enormous shadow fell over Sinbad.
The brave sailor looked up. The shadow was made
by a gigantic bird. She was about to land on her
gigantic egg! Sinbad was scared.

Again, Scheherryzade stopped. But the Queen wanted to know what happened next, so she made Scheherryzade promise to go on with the story tomorrow.

The next night Scheherryzade returned to the palace and went on with his tale. It went like this:

As soon as Sinbad saw the gigantic bird, he turned and ran away as fast as he could!

Just when Sinbad felt he could run no more, he looked up and saw a huge, scary monster. The monster's name was Cyclops.

With his huge, hairy hand Cyclops thrust a giant yo-yo at Sinbad. He wanted Sinbad to help wind the string. The brave sailor was glad to help.

Around and around the giant yo-yo Sinbad ran, winding the string as he went. When it was all wound, Cyclops thanked Sinbad.

Just at that moment, Sinbad spied something incredible! It was so incredible that Sinbad started jumping up and down and hollering.

Again Scheherryzade yawned and stopped the story. The Queen whined and begged. She offered Scheherryzade anything to finish the tale. She even offered to take back her command banning bedtime stories!

Scheherryzade's plan had worked! Because the Queen took back her grouchy law, Scheherryzade gladly finished the story of Sinbad.

It went like this:

The incredible thing Sinbad spied was— a ship! Sinbad waved wildly, and the ship came to rescue him. Brave Sinbad sailed home and lived happily ever after.

For once the grouchy Queen was happy. She loved
Scheherryzade's story.

So the Queen had it proclaimed far and wide that bedtime stories were no longer forbidden!

Bedtime stories were told once again throughout the land. Scheherryzade was a hero!